THIS BOOK BELONGS TO:

Jack and Ellie

"Maybe one day, you'll write a book about your adventures, too!"

Publisher's note: This book is a work of fiction. Names, characters, places and incidents either are the product of the author's imagination or are used fictitiously, and any resemblance to actual persons or animals living or dead, events, or locales is entirely coincidental.

Request for permission to make copies of any part of the work should be mailed to the following address:
Permission Department, TriMark Press, Inc., 368 South Military Trail, Deerfield Beach, Florida 33442
800-889-0693

Library of Congress Cataloging-in-Publications Data is available
Haley Marguerite Mariano
Illustrated by Daniel J. Montenegro
Charlie Takes an Adventure

ISBN: 978-1-943401-06-2
Library of Congress Control Number: 2015952305
A16
First Edition
10 9 8 7 6 5 4 3 2 1

For further information, please contact the publisher:

368 South Military Trail
Deerfield Beach, FL 33442
800-889-0693
www.TriMarkPress.com

O nce upon a time there was an adventurous penguin named

CHARLES IGNATIUS ADELIE.

Sit right back and relax because I'm about tell you a story of the penguin that we call "Charlie."

CHARLIE TAKES AN ADVENTURE

Charlie lives in the ancient city of Urdz. Urdz is located in Antarctica, where it is extremely cold.

Charlie's home is in the section of town called Pickering Warf. He doesn't like "The Warf" because he thinks there is nothing to do and no one to play with.

Winter lasts a really long time in Antarctica. The days are really short and the nights are very long. It's so cold in Antarctica that if you're not careful, your eyeballs can freeze.

Now, Charlie is a penguin, and he is supposed to like the cold weather.

But Charlie doesn't like it at all. What is he supposed to do?

CHARLIE TAKES AN ADVENTURE

So one day, while Charlie was waiting to get a haircut, he decided to look at some travel magazines that were left on the table.

He grabbed the magazine that had palm trees and beaches on the cover. It was a travel magazine about Florida. Charlie read every word about traveling to Florida. It said, "The weather is sunny and warm, the people are really nice, and there are plenty of things to do."

After reading all of the wonderful things about Florida, Charlie decided it was time for him to go!

The very next day, Charlie set out on a plane to Florida where there's warm weather, plenty of activities, and a whole lot of people to be with…

CHARLIE TAKES AN ADVENTURE

Shortly after Charlie took his seat on the plane, the flight attendant said, "Everyone please fasten your seatbelt."

Charlie had never been on a plane before. He wasn't sure what a seatbelt was. But Charlie watched the other passengers and figured out how to put it on.

Ten minutes after they were up in the air, the flight attendant spoke again: "Snacks and beverages will be served in a few minutes." When she came with the snacks and beverages, Charlie had his headphones on and was listening to music.

The flight attendant asked Charlie, "What can I get for you?"

He responded, "Fish." The lady sitting next to Charlie with the pink polka dot dress just stared at him for a very long time.

CHARLIE TAKES AN ADVENTURE

When Charlie stepped off the plane in Florida, he thought to himself, "Hello Sunshine!"

The weather was sunny and warm, just like the magazine said it would be.

Charlie then took a cab to the Palm Bay Hotel in Coconut Grove.

As the porter helped Charlie with his bags, he noticed that the bags were really heavy and had a horrible, rancid odor coming from within them.

Charlie explained that they were full of raw fish and mahi-mahi sushi, his favorite entrée to eat. He brought them with him from Antarctica. Unfortunately, the warm weather was not good for Charlie's food…

CHARLIE TAKES AN ADVENTURE

Later that day, Charlie decided to go to Miami Beach for a swim.

When he arrived at the beach, Charlie observed a sign that read, "Sea lice today… NO swimming."

Charlie was a bit disappointed but assumed he could at least lie down and get a sun tan.

Within minutes, the sky became dark and it started to rain like cats and dogs!

CHARLIE TAKES AN ADVENTURE

That night, Charlie thought it might be enjoyable to go to a party downstairs in the lobby of the hotel, so he could spend time with some new people. One of the reasons for Charlie's adventure was to meet new people, remember?

So when Charlie arrived in the lobby, it seemed that everyone was delighted to see him. This made Charlie smile. After about ten minutes of walking around the party and mingling with the other guests, an elegantly dressed lady approached Charlie and asked him to bring her a Shirley Temple.

Charlie had no problem doing this because he thought that perhaps she admired him. Charlie thought to himself, "This is great!"

CHARLIE TAKES AN ADVENTURE

On Charlie's way back to the elegantly dressed lady, with her glass in hand, three other people asked for the exact same thing. Charlie felt he was very popular and that made him extremely happy.

When Charlie dropped off the last glass, the gentleman said to Charlie, "It's always nice to have good help at these parties." Charlie replied, "I'm not a waiter! I'm just another person here at the party."

The man replied, "You look like a waiter… you are wearing a tuxedo, aren't you?"

Charlie ran out from the party crying because he believed everyone was being nice to him because he was a guest, not a waiter.

CHARLIE TAKES AN ADVENTURE

The next morning, Charlie set out for Happy World because it was the happiest place on the planet Earth.

He had read that there were roller coasters, water slides, haunted houses and plenty more fun rides.

Charlie purchased his ticket and ran to get in line to go on the water slide first, since it was wicked hot outside.

Cooling off on this ride would be ideal before hitting the rest of the park!

CHARLIE TAKES AN ADVENTURE

Charlie had waited in line for an hour and a half and was losing his patience while dripping with sweat.

When he got to the front of the line, he was told by the man working there, "The water slide just broke and needs to be fixed. It will be at least three and a half hours… sorry, come back later."

Charlie was sooooo disappointed.

CHARLIE TAKES AN ADVENTURE

Next, Charlie decided to go on the "Outer Space" roller coaster.

Luckily, there was a much shorter line, only a fifteen minute wait.

Charlie loved roller coasters. The magazine said this roller coaster was one of the best ever!

When Charlie reached the front of the line, the person working there said, "I am sorry, sir, but you're much too short for this ride. You must be at least four feet tall to go on this ride."

Charlie was only two and a half feet tall.

Unfortunately for Charlie, this happened every time he tried to go on a ride.

CHARLIE TAKES AN ADVENTURE

Disappointed, hot and lonely, Charlie decided to leave "The World's Happiest Place."

As Charlie was driving away from the park, he noticed a sign on the road that said: "Fortune Teller — All wishes come true."

Charlie parked his car in the parking lot and walked towards the gate to the fortune teller's yard.

He opened up the gate and walked through a garden which led him down a path to the fortune teller.

The fortune teller, who called herself Maya, looked up at Charlie and smiled… and told him to sit down.

CHARLIE TAKES AN ADVENTURE

Maya looked at Charlie with piercing eyes and asked him, "What's wrong, dear?"

"I need a person who can grant me a wish," said Charlie. "It's very important to me."

The fortune teller smiled and said, "You've come to the right place…"

"So, Charlie, how may I help you?" asked Maya.

Charlie told Maya, "I left Antarctica to go to Florida because I was bored, I had no one to play with, and I had nothing to do."

Maya looked into her crystal ball before she gave him this answer…

CHARLIE TAKES AN ADVENTURE

Maya told Charlie about an old Slovakian proverb that goes just like this...

"Do not look for apples under a poplar tree."

Charlie just sat there, trying to figure out what that meant...

After a minute or two, Charlie realized what Maya was trying to tell him. She was telling him that...

"You don't really need to go elsewhere...
to find what you really want in life...
you can find it right in your own backyard."

27

CHARLIE TAKES AN ADVENTURE

This made Charlie really happy because he knew what he had to do.

"I cannot waste another minute," Charlie said. "I have to go back to my family and friends in Antarctica!"

Charlie immediately packed his bags and headed to the airport.

The plane ride home was long. It takes almost twenty hours to get there from Florida.

Charlie was so excited when the plane arrived at the Antarctica airport!

CHARLIE TAKES AN ADVENTURE

Waiting for Charlie at the airport was his family and friends. Many held signs that said, "Welcome home!" and "We missed you!"

Charlie told his family and friends, "I'll never leave you guys again. I missed you all so very much." Charlie's family and friends all gave Charlie a big group hug. This made Charlie feel very wanted and missed.

When they were done with the group hug, Charlie told his mother that he was hungry. It was a long trip, you know.

Charlie's mom asked Charlie, "What would you like to eat, my dear?"

Charlie replied, "Well… fish!" From that day forward, Charlie lived in Antarctica happily ever after with his family and friends.

ABOUT THE ILLUSTRATOR

Daniel J. Montenegro is a 2015 alumnus of Design and Architecture Senior High in Miami, Florida, where he studied graphic design. He is pursuing a BFA in Illustration at the School of Visual Arts in New York, New York. In addition to being part of the 2014 Young Designers Consortium SVA Pre-college Program, he has entered work in the 2014 Mountain Dew Green Label Gallery in Amsterdam and was a 2015 National Young Arts Finalist (Merit Award) and a 2015 Scholastics Gold Key Portfolio winner (Regional).

Artist's Statement: *"The purpose of my work is simply to entertain others. I'm constantly sharing my work with my peers, mostly uploading images online, hoping that people smile and laugh in response, as it is the intention of the majority of the pieces I create. The characters I create are my children and like any parent, I wish for my children to bring smiles to everyone they meet."*

ABOUT THE AUTHOR

Haley Marguerite Mariano, a Lynn University graduate, holds a Bachelor of Fine Arts degree in Multimedia Journalism. She is a self-driven entrepreneur and in her free time, she may be writing children's books, running along Boca Raton's beautiful Spanish River Beach, or volunteering in the greater Palm Beach County. She holds affiliations with the American Cancer Society, Boca Helping Hands, and Hospice by the Sea.

Accomplished with the spoken and written word, Haley has years of Toastmasters International experience. This vivacious author is the face behind Social Inspired Leader, which has developed a large following. Join Haley (and Charlie!) as she "takes the adventure" of a motivational speaking career at www.SocialInspiredLeader.com.

THANK YOU

First, I would like to thank my father, Anthony Mariano, for giving me the idea to write this book when I was in the sixth grade, always believing in me, and never giving up on me. Thank you to my mother, Laurie Mariano, for her love and unconditional support. Another important person I would like to thank is Isabella Vengoechea Abuchaibe for leading me in the right direction and helping me find the perfect illustrator. Last but certainly not least, Daniel J. Montenegro, my illustrator. I couldn't have done it without you. Your willingness to help me with this children's book went over and beyond, exceeding my expectations each and every time. I wish you all the best. Congrats to us both on our first children's book!!!

—Haley Marguerite Mariano
SocialInspiredLeader.com

WHERE WILL CHARLIE GO NEXT?

Write a story about Charlie's next adventure on the lines below.
Then share it with a buddy!

_____

_____

_____

_____

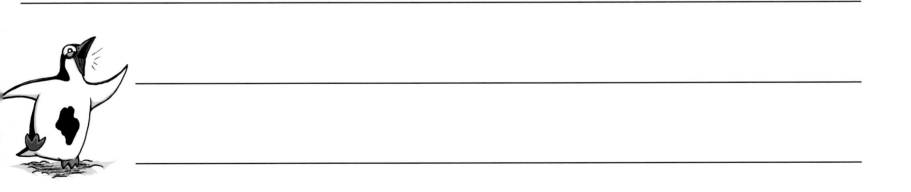

_____

WHERE WILL CHARLIE GO NEXT?

Draw an illustration of Charlie's next adventure in the space below.
Then share it with a buddy!